Mythical Creatures

BIGFOOT

by Molly Jones

FOCUS READERS

FOCUS READERS

www.focusreaders.com

Focus Readers is distributed by North Star Editions:
sales@northstareditions.com | 888-417-0195

Produced for Focus Readers by Red Line Editorial.

Photographs ©: aleks1949/Shutterstock Images, cover, 1; RichLegg/iStockphoto, 4–5; KatieDobies/iStockphoto, 7; wildpixel/iStockphoto, 8–9, 29; pabradyphoto/iStockphoto, 10; RikoBest/Shutterstock Images, 13; Artush/Shutterstock Images, 14–15; Onyx9/Shutterstock Images, 16–17; Bill Schaefer/The Idaho State Journal/AP Images, 18; Lloyd Young/AP Images, 21; CSNafzger/Shutterstock Images, 22–23; RichVintage/iStockphoto, 25; Sheri Wake/Shutterstock Images, 26

ISBN
978-1-63517-899-9 (hardcover)
978-1-64185-001-8 (paperback)
978-1-64185-203-6 (ebook pdf)
978-1-64185-102-2 (hosted ebook)

Library of Congress Control Number: 2018931699

Printed in the United States of America
Mankato, MN
May, 2018

About the Author

Molly Jones is the author of 15 books for young readers. She enjoys writing about history, health and medicine, and controversial issues. She lives on Lake Murray in South Carolina, where she likes to sail, walk, read, and practice yoga.

TABLE OF CONTENTS

CHAPTER 1

WINTER IN THE WOODS

Bigfoot stretches and yawns. The cold January air seeps into his family's cave. He tries not to wake his **mate** or child. Like him, they are hungry. Food is scarce at this time of year. Bushes are empty.

In some stories, Bigfoot lives alone. In others, he has a family.

Bears picked every berry, nut, and root before sleeping for the winter.

Bigfoot is thirsty, too. But he doesn't want to be seen by humans. Even the short trip to the stream is risky. He waits until he's sure the coast is clear.

FUN FACT

In 1941, hunters in Illinois spotted a creature they thought was Bigfoot. The creature escaped by leaping 20 to 40 feet (6 to 12 m) at a time.

A sign warns hikers of possible Bigfoot sightings.

CHAPTER 2

A LARGE LEGEND

People have reported Bigfoot sightings for years. Some claim they have seen the ape-like creature. Others think they have spotted his footprint.

Most Bigfoot sightings occur in forests or woods.

The names Sasquatch and Bigfoot are both used to describe the same mythical creature.

Many parts of the world have **legends** of a huge, hairy beast. In North America, native people told stories of a wild man. The legend continued as settlers came from Europe. In 1811, a man in Canada found large footprints in the snow. Later, other Canadians said they saw the creature. The monster became known as Sasquatch.

In the United States, the creature was named Bigfoot. Many sightings occurred in the Pacific Northwest.

FUN FACT

Hawaii is the only US state without any Bigfoot sightings.

People claimed to see the creature walking in forests.

A similar creature also exists in Asian **folklore**. In these stories, the creature lives in snowy mountains. His name is the Yeti.

Many people have tried to find Bigfoot. They make **casts** of the

FUN FACT

In the 1970s, many people reported seeing **UFOs**. They thought Bigfoot and UFOs might be connected.

The Yeti is said to live in the Himalayan Mountains.

footprints they find. Some take photos and videos. Scientists think these are fake. So far, no one has proved the monster to be real.

EXPLORING THE MYTH

BIGFOOT TODAY

Bigfoot is popular today. A TV show on Animal Planet follows the hunt for Bigfoot. The creature is also the hero of the Disney movie *Bigfoot*.

Many people still look for Bigfoot. The Bigfoot Field Research Organization seeks to learn more about Bigfoot. People want to learn about the Yeti, too. In western China, scientists studied Yeti **samples**. One sample was a piece of skin. Some people thought the sample came from the Yeti's hand. Scientists proved them wrong. They found that the sample came from a bear.

Yeti samples helped scientists learn about Himalayan bears.

CHAPTER 3

HALF HUMAN, HALF APE

Based on sightings, Bigfoot is tall, hairy, and brown. Some report him to be as tall as 9 feet (2.7 m). Bigfoot is heavy, too. He weighs more than 600 pounds (272 kg).

Bigfoot is thought to be larger than an average-sized gorilla.

A natural history museum collected casts of Bigfoot's footprint.

Similar to an ape, he has thick hair over his whole body.

However, Bigfoot also has human traits. Similar to a human, Bigfoot walks on two legs. But his feet are larger than human feet. Most Bigfoot prints are 16 to 18 inches (41 to 46 cm) long. Some are as wide as 7 inches (18 cm).

Bigfoot's footprints could be proof that the creature exists. Some prints show small lines and ridges. These details are different than a human's foot. Other prints have only three or four toes. Some people think a print with these details could not be a **hoax**.

Scientists have studied Bigfoot samples. Some samples were strands of hair. Scientists proved that the hairs were not from Bigfoot. Instead, the hairs came from humans and animals. Many of the hairs came from bears. Some hikers mistake bears for Bigfoot.

FUN FACT

Some people say the Yeti has reversed feet. His big toe is on the outside of his foot.

A scientist studies hair samples that could belong to Bigfoot.

CHAPTER 4

THE BEHAVIOR OF BIGFOOT

Some people who see Bigfoot say he acts like a human. Others say he acts like an ape. For example, Bigfoot does not use words to speak. Instead, he makes a loud, animal-like scream.

Sometimes, people dress up like Bigfoot to trick others.

The most famous footage of Bigfoot is known as the Patterson film. The 1967 film shows a creature walking through a forest. The creature's gait is different than a human's. It lifts its legs higher. The figure is also hunched over. The film matches other Bigfoot

FUN FACT

Bigfoot's diet is a mystery. Some people think he eats meat. Others think he only eats plants.

Most films or photos of Bigfoot are blurry.

sightings. But many people believe the film is fake.

Some people think the scratch marks on this tree in Maryland came from Bigfoot.

So far, there is no **evidence** that Bigfoot is real. Scientists argue that a human-like species would use tools. For example, Bigfoot might use tools to hunt. But no one has ever found proof of these tools. Scientists study **fossils** to learn about animals that have died. But no one has ever found a Bigfoot fossil. No one has found a body of a Bigfoot that died, either. Until then, Bigfoot remains a **myth**.

FUN FACT

US President Teddy Roosevelt liked to hunt. Some people said he once shot a Bigfoot. But the story was not true.

FOCUS ON
BIGFOOT

Write your answers on a separate piece of paper.

1. Write a one-sentence summary of Chapter 2.

2. Do you think Bigfoot exists? Why or why not?

3. Why is Bigfoot believed to be a myth?

- **A.** No one has ever claimed to see the creature.
- **B.** Scientists have not found fossils of the creature.
- **C.** A creature as large as Bigfoot could not survive on Earth.

4. What is the main difference between Bigfoot and the Yeti?

- **A.** Bigfoot is from North America, and the Yeti is from Asia.
- **B.** The Yeti is related to Sasquatch, and Bigfoot is not.
- **C.** The Yeti has more human features than Bigfoot.

5. What does **footage** mean in this book?

*The most famous **footage** of Bigfoot is known as the Patterson film. The 1967 film shows a creature walking through a forest.*

A. a video recording

B. a journey taken on foot

C. a fictional story

6. What does **gait** mean in this book?

*The creature's **gait** is different than a human's. It lifts its legs higher.*

A. tone of voice

B. place for sleeping

C. way of walking

Answer key on page 32.

GLOSSARY

casts
Models of objects made by shaping material into molds.

evidence
Facts or pieces of information that prove something is true.

folklore
Fictional stories that people pass down over the years.

fossils
Parts of an animal or plant that remain preserved in rock.

hoax
A trick or prank.

legends
Well-known stories from the past that are often untrue.

mate
A partner that an animal has babies with.

myth
A well-known, fictional story common to a group of people.

samples
Small pieces taken from a larger object or living thing for study.

UFOs
Short for "unidentified flying objects." UFOs are mysterious things that appear in the sky.

TO LEARN MORE

BOOKS

Hall, Brianna. *Hair-Raising Monster Stories*. North Mankato, MN: Capstone Press, 2014.

Nagle, Frances. *Bigfoot*. New York: Gareth Stevens Publishing, 2017.

Rivkin, Jennifer. *Searching for Bigfoot*. New York: PowerKids Press, 2015.

NOTE TO EDUCATORS

Visit **www.focusreaders.com** to find lesson plans, activities, links, and other resources related to this title.

INDEX

Answer Key: 1. Answers will vary; **2.** Answers will vary; **3.** B; **4.** A; **5.** A; **6.** C